WHAT'S ANANSI UP TO NOW!

Gillena Cox

AuthorHouse™ UK
1663 Liberty Drive
Bloomington, IN 47403 USA
www.authorhouse.co.uk
Phone: 0800 047 8203 (Domestic TFN)
+44 1908 723714 (International)

Because of the dynamic nature of the Internet, any web addresses or links contained in this book may have changed since publication and may no longer be valid. The views expressed in this work are solely those of the author and do not necessarily reflect the views of the publisher, and the publisher hereby disclaims any responsibility for them.

Any people depicted in stock imagery provided by Getty Images are models, and such images are being used for illustrative purposes only.
Certain stock imagery © Getty Images.

This book is printed on acid-free paper.

ISBN: 978-1-7283-9870-9 (sc)
ISBN: 978-1-7283-9869-3 (e)

Print information available on the last page.

Published by AuthorHouse 02/11/2020

authorHOUSE®

Introduction

This is the third time we are guests of the Anansi family. On this occasion, Anansi is faced with a dilemma of sorts. No gifts to the Children for Christmas! Can he do this?

Again, I crave your indulgence dear readers, as I present Anansi in a new light, like I have done throughout this series

Delightful reading hours to all!

Contents

Dedication

To all lovers of Parang and 'Nancy Stories

Christmas Eve

a box shaken well -
bits of stuffing no one wants
scatter on the floor

It was night time, dark night, almost as dark as that silent holy night of long, long, ago. Really, it was Christmas Eve. Anansi who was taking a nap, got up from his bed, to scurry past on tiptoes. Mrs. Anansi in the kitchen, was too swamped with the delicious smells from her breads, cakes and cookies baking; and of course, the pleasant humming of her favourite, all time classic carol, The Twelve Days of Christmas, to hear her husband slip by and leave the house.

Earlier in the year, they (Mr. and Mrs. Anansi), had decided not to buy their children any Christmas gifts. They both had come to the decision that their children were just too spoilt.

They sneaked under the Christmas tree on Christmas Eve night shaking all the boxes, peeking here and peeking there. They opened gifts after Christmas morning mass, barely even wanting to have breakfast. They had to be called three, and four, and five times, to sit down and have some breakfast.

They would open their gifts, and after all the boxes were open, they looked to make sure there were no more left to open and then they turned over and shook the already opened boxes, before they started to play. After that, the house would be filled with squeals, giggles, and laughter, throughout the day. Not to mention the varied sounds from different kinds of electronic toys.

Christmas Tree Grande

red Poinsettias
distorted by the breezes -
billowing curtains

Gorgeous new curtains adorned the living room, which she Mrs. Anansi had chosen, bought, and put up, all by herself. Beautiful patterned poinsettia panels. She loved a splash of red at Christmas time.

In a corner of the Anansi living room, there stood a giant Christmas tree, all ribboned, and sparkling, and tinselled, and baubled, and beaded, and colourful, and sad! Yes! the Anansi family Christmas tree was a sad tree. Has the Anansi household, in the sunny Caribbean, suddenly gone colder than winter?

Then, how come Mrs. Anansi still hummed her favourite Christmas carol " on the first day of Christmas my true love gave to me la la la la la la la la." And, what of Anansi? why this sneaking about on such a night? What's Anansi up to now?

Well! a good two hours or so had passed, without Anansi returning, while Mrs. Anansi continued humming, though her baking was finished. In her Christmas reverie, she headed for the living room striding towards the Christmas tree.

What's this? Is she planning to string popcorn to the tree?

Chirarr Chirarr

the artist's fancy -
three magi may stand or kneel
Nativity scenes

Well meanwhile, Anansi having tripped, and rolled, about three times in the dark, thought he heard crickets and cicadas laughing at him. "Silly Anansi" he though he heard them saying. "The three magi traveled, far and wide, days and nights, to bring gifts to the baby Jesus where his mother had laid him in the manger". "Silly Anansi Chirarr Chirarr"

Oh no I am imagining things, thought Anansi. Don't crickets and cicadas sleep this time of night? And he continued moving through the bush. "Silly Anancy!" he thought he heard them saying again. "Didn't Saint Nicholas leave gifts and offerings to children long long long long time ago when he was alive?" "Silly Anansi Chirarr Chirarr," sounded again.

Poor Anansi, by then he had gotten to his favourite rock, where he often times came to ponder things. Or, when he got together with his pals in the rainforest, to lime. Here they talked and argued about floods, and hurricanes, and tsunamis, and snow storms, and such like: the ways of the environment fascinated them. These were manly topics, they thought. By then, they would have forgotten the grocery lists their wives had given to them, returning home empty handed; only to be scolded by their wives.

Night of Wonder

*the new family
angels acclaim them -
a night so holy*

Oh yes! Anansi had his flaws. And to this place in the forest is were, he came to ponder, many times, with a heart heavy with sadness, having been scolded by Mrs. Anansi. However, at these times, Wind stroked his spidery cheeks, and the rustle of the leaves soothed him.

Remember though; this was Christmas Eve night. A night of heightened expectancy, a Night of Wonder and ethereal promise, a night; busy with angelic voices practising their singing. So, it was by no means strange to hear voices on such a night. Even voices whispering to Anansi; who some say, was a super-hero kind of being, who could walk upright like men do, but at the same time he could spin webs and traverse distances, ordinary men could not.

But, that's beside the point. Anansi shook himself up straight, gathered up the bag of toys he had hidden in the forest and headed for home. He would just have to make Mrs. Anansi understand, he mused. He just couldn't do it, he couldn't not-buy his children gifts for Christmas.

Oops!

he the pivot
of all the festivities -
baby Jesus

When he got back to his house, the living room was just barely lit, so on tiptoes, he approached the Christmas tree and placed his stash of gifts under. Then, backing away slowly, feeling very pleased with what he had done...OOPs! he bumped into Mrs. Anansi, who was also on tippy toes.

Spilling from her, was a good arm full of gifts. They looked at each other in the dimly lit living room, what seemed like, a good five seconds. Then, they both burst out laughing.

Anansi held out his empty arms to Mrs. Anansi. She in turn hugged him. "Mistletoe" said Mrs. Anansi smiling, as she produced a sprig of plastic Mistletoe as if by magic, holding it high over their heads. They kissed good night, and she immediately starting humming again - on the twelfth day of Christmas my true love gave to me la la la la la la la, as they retrieved the spilled packages; wrapped, and ribboned, placing then carefully under their awesome Christmas tree.

THE END

I wish you dear readers a Merry Christmas and
a Bright and Prosperous New Year

A Few Words Explained

Haibun: a Japanese literary form using prose and haiku

Haiku: Plural also haiku, a very tiny poem of Japanese origin. In English, usually presented in 3 lines in a total of not more than 17 syllables, capturing and storing a moment, some may consider just ordinary.

Lime: A get together with friends.

'nancy story: A story about Anansi The Spider

Poinsettias: also known as the Christmas flower. Actually, the coloured showy bracts are what gets our attention.

About The Author

 Gillena Cox lives in St James, Trinidad of The Republic of Trinidad and Tobago. A retired Library Assistant. Amateur writer/artist/ photographer; dabbling in poetry and children's stories, art, nature photos, and as well blogging, writing and interacting within online poetry and art communities – her hobbies.

Born 1950. Married in 1971. A mother and grandmother.

Favourite Christmas tree ornament - The star

Other Books By This Author

Moments – 100 haiku poems 2007 [Adult]

Pink Crush – A book of poems 2011 [Adult]

The Little Seed and His Brother 2015 [Children]

Under the Chinaberry Tree 2016 [Children]

Third Planet from The Sun 2017 [Children]

Anansi And The Twelve Days Of Christmas 2018
[Children - Chapter Book, Book 1]

Anansi An Unusual Experience 2019 [Children - Chapter Book, Book 2]

Series Note

First in this series was 'Anansi And the Twelve Days Of Christmas ' this story appeared in draft at my blog Lunch Break in a collaboration titled 'The Twelve days of Christmas' from December 25th 2011 to January 5th 2012.

Second in this series was 'Anansi An Unusual Experience' which appeared in draft at my blog Lunch Break in the collaboration 'The Twelve days of Christmas' from December 25th 2012 to January 5th 2013.

And finally, this story 'What's Anancy Up To Now' which appeared in draft at my blog Lunch Break in the collaboration 'The Twelve days of Christmas' from December 25th 2013 to January 5th 2014.

In the blog collaboration, friends were invited to share Christmas poems, and images. None of the works of any of these participants are included in these three books of this Anansi mini-series. However, thanks is due to friends, for their appreciation and encouragement, those who participated at my Lunch Break postings; in the draft presentations.

Printed in the United States
By Bookmasters